Abracadabra!

Shanshan Li

illustrated by **Sifan Yang**

Spider went to visit his friend Caterpillar.

Caterpillar hid in her small house.

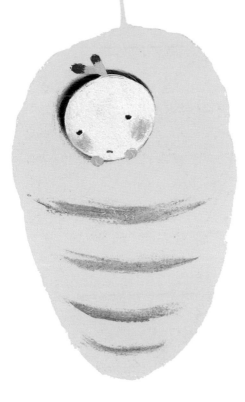

"Can you come out?"
Caterpillar shook her head.

"Are you sick?"
Caterpillar shook her head again.

"Are you not happy?"
Once again, Caterpillar shook
her head.

"How can I make my friend happy?"
Spider asked himself.

He got an idea and climbed up his web.

Spider came back with leaves and flowers.

"Let me perform some magic. I'm good at it!"

"Abracadabra..."

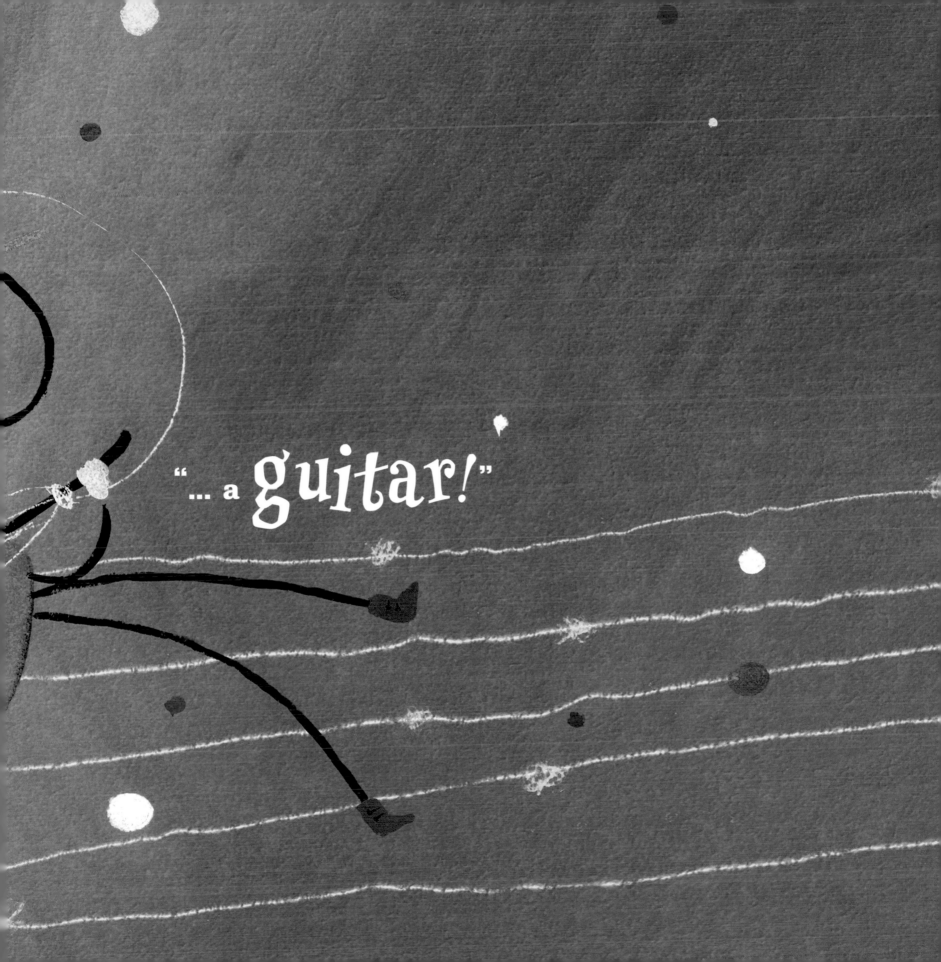

"... a guitar!"

"How do you like it?" asked Spider proudly.
Caterpillar looked at him, but said nothing.

"Well, I will show you something even more interesting..."

"Abracadabra!"

"a necklace!"

"a skirt!"

"These are for you. How do you like them?"

Caterpillar kept her head down, without a word.

"Maybe I should show you something even more wonderful..."

"Abracadabra!"

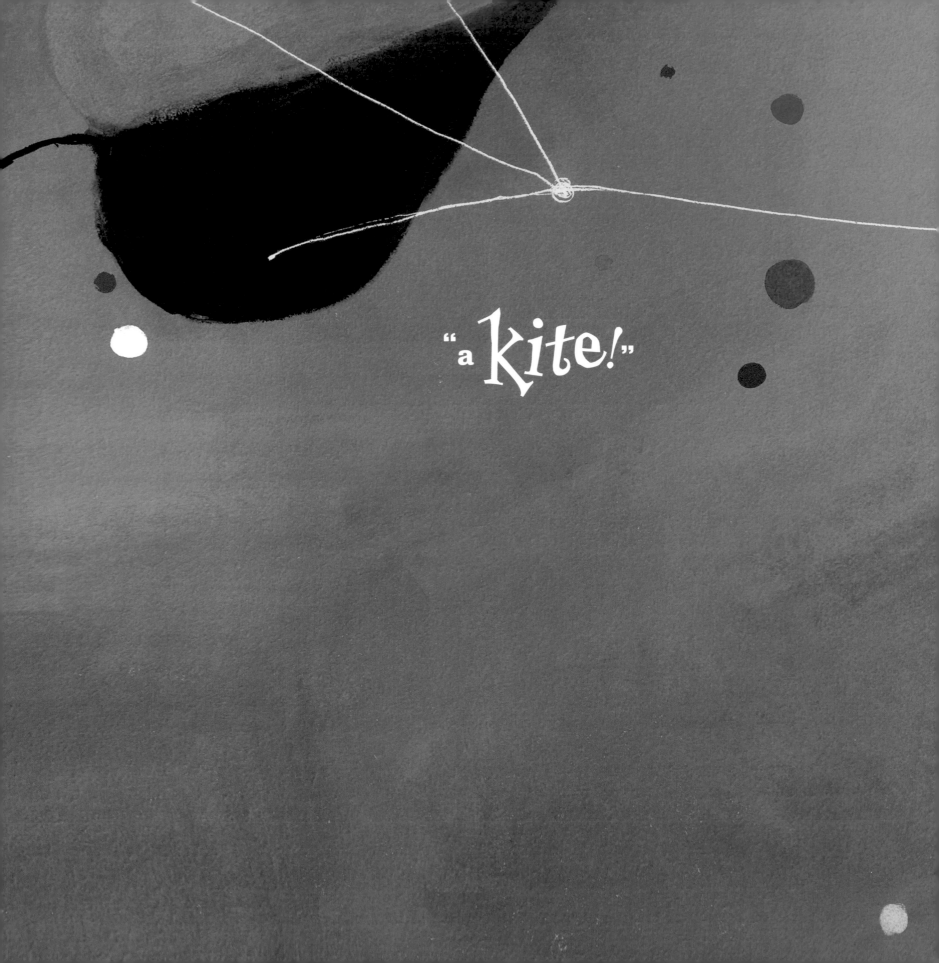

"a kite!"

"a swing!"

"a **paraglider!**"

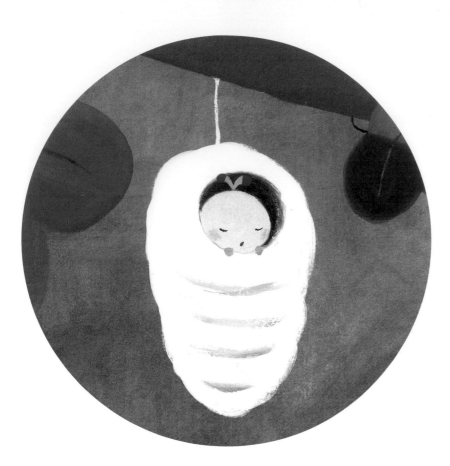

Caterpillar didn't say anything.
She squinted her eyes and sat silently.

"Okay, this time it must be a real eye-opener!"
"Attention, please..."

"Abracadabra!"

"twinkling **stars!**"

"a shining **moon!**"

"and a golden **sun!**"

Spider came closer to Caterpillar.

"Look, your sun is smiling!"

To his surprise,
Caterpillar had fallen asleep.

"I have done so many tricks,"
said Spider sadly.
"Well, I've got to go."

Spider then turned to give
Caterpillar another look.
She seemed as if she
would not wake up
anytime soon.

Caterpillar
kept
sleeping
for
a
long,
long
time.

One day, Spider returned
to Caterpillar's house.

Caterpillar popped part of her head out.
"A moment, please," she said shyly.

Slowly she crawled out
and whispered...

"a b r a c a d a b r a . . ."

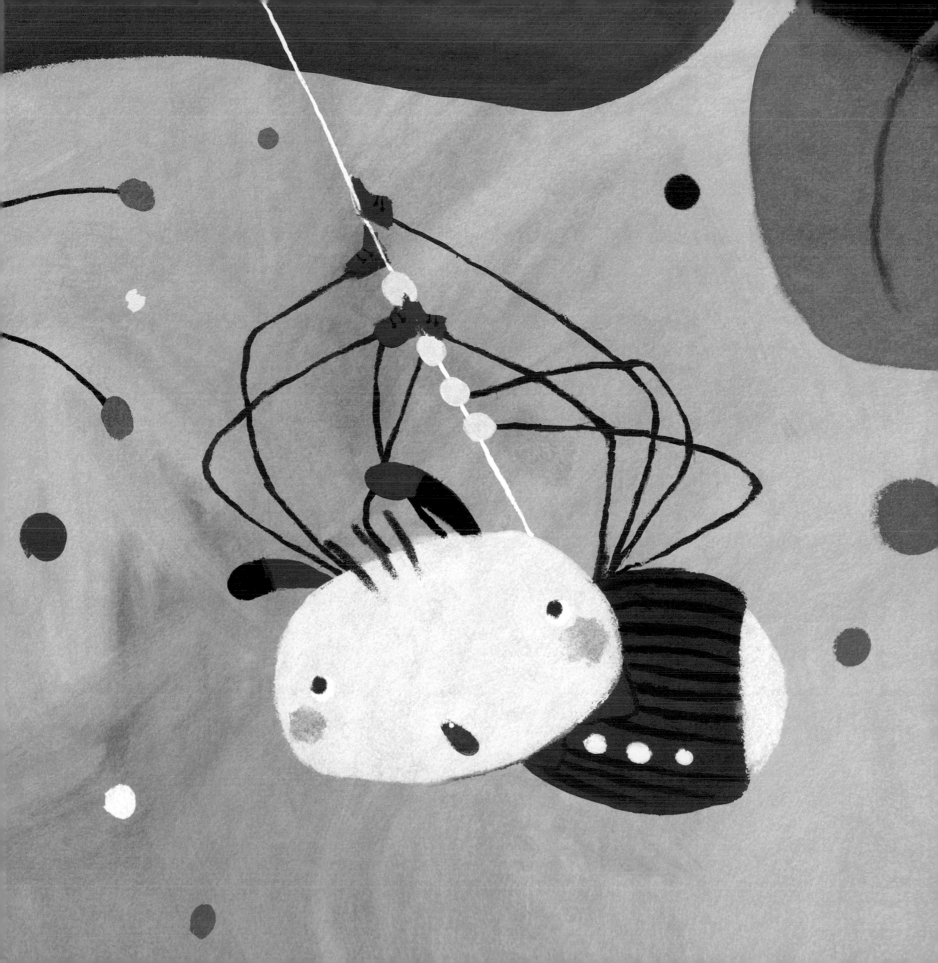

Caterpillar had turned into
a beautiful butterfly!

Shanshan Li

Shanshan Li is an international award-winning author of more than sixty books, fairy tales, and poems for children. When she's not writing she serves as the Director of China's Children's Literature Research Institute and is a member of the China Writer's Association.

Sifan Yang

Sifan Yang has illustrated hundreds of children's books and written fifteen picture books. He enjoys bringing his unique personal style to his work.